Published in the United States by Random House Children's Books, a division of Penguin Random House LLC, 1745 Broadway, New York, NY 10019, and in Canada by Penguin Random House Canada Limited, Toronto. Random House and the colophon are registered trademarks of Penguin Random House LLC.

ISBN 978-0-593-31043-4 (trade) — ISBN 978-0-593-31044-1 (ebook)

Printed in the United States of America

10 9 8 7 6 5 4 3 2 1

Random House Children's Books supports the First Amendment and celebrates the right to read.

THE BATMAN™

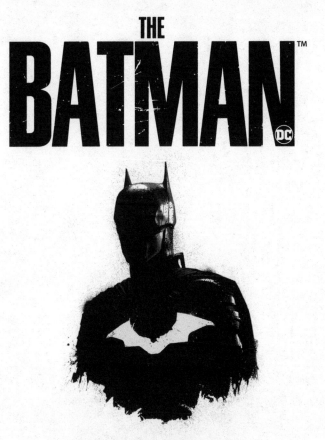

Before The Batman: An Original Movie Novel

The high-octane prequel story to *The Batman*

**Special Edition Movie Novel
By David Lewman**

Batman created by Bob Kane with Bill Finger

Random House  New York

Part One

Prologue

THE BOY IN THE CHOIR

Bruce felt strange being back in the old house.

He and his parents had lived in the mansion, Wayne Manor, until he was six years old. Then they'd donated their sprawling home to Gotham City to serve as an orphanage and moved into their current residence, Wayne Tower.

Now he was ten years old, and his father, Thomas Wayne, was running for mayor. His dad had decided to announce his candidacy at the orphanage. So Bruce and his parents had returned to their former home for a visit.

As they climbed the grand staircase to the second floor, Bruce remembered playing on the stairs. He saw the door to a closet and recalled crouching behind the hanging coats for a game of hide-and-seek, waiting for his mother to find him, laughing. It was a big house, full of great places to hide. Even though he liked their new home in Wayne Tower, Bruce realized he missed the old house. He'd been happy there. Seeing it again, he felt a kind of ache.

Upstairs, in what had once been a ballroom, the orphanage's choir stood on risers, singing a medley of patriotic songs. The Waynes had called the long hall "the party room," only using it when they entertained large numbers of guests. But when it was empty, Bruce had played in the big room, rolling toy race cars across the gleaming wooden floor all by himself. The floor didn't seem as shiny now as it had then, when it reflected the light from the sparkling chandeliers hanging overhead. Bruce glanced up. The chandeliers had been replaced with sturdier, more practical light fixtures. They were a little dusty.

TV cameras were set up to capture his father's announcement for the evening news. Reporters from newspapers and magazines waited with recorders and notepads. Photographers snapped pictures. Thomas Wayne's campaign manager handed out copies of his remarks. Orphanage staff members looked around nervously, hoping everything would go smoothly. The residents had been warned repeatedly to be on their very best behavior.

The medley came to an end. The woman conducting the choir turned toward the cameras and smiled. There was scattered applause from the small group gathered for the candidate's announcement. The reporters weren't sure how to react to the music. They'd come for a news event, not a concert.

Now that the orphans had stopped watching their conductor, Bruce felt as though they were all staring at him. *There's the rich kid who used to live here,* they were probably all thinking. *The billionaire's son.* Bruce wanted to look away, stare at the floor. But he knew his parents were counting on him to make a good impression, so he looked back at the kids in the choir. They're weren't all looking at him, too excited by the TV cameras and photographers to care that much about a ten-year-old kid in an expensive suit.

Except for one boy.

He was scrawny, with aviator-style wire-rimmed glasses. His clothes seemed a little too big. They were hand-me-downs he hadn't grown into yet. And he was looking straight at Bruce. *Why is he staring at me?* Bruce thought. *Do I look weird or something?* He wished the kid would look away. But then he felt sorry for the guy, living in an orphanage without any parents. Even though he didn't really feel like smiling, Bruce forced himself to give the kid a friendly smile.

The kid continued to stare. He didn't smile back.

Chapter One

SUMMER PLANS

Seven years later, Bruce Wayne climbed out of the back seat of a long black limousine parked in front of Wayne Tower. The driver popped the trunk and hurried to fetch Bruce's luggage, but the seventeen-year-old beat him to it. "I got it," Bruce said, lifting the leather bags out of the trunk.

"Are you sure, sir?" the driver asked.

"Yeah," Bruce said. "Thanks."

"You're welcome," the driver said. "It must feel good to be home."

Bruce grunted. Did it feel good to be home? He wasn't sure. He didn't love the private boarding school he attended, but he didn't exactly love his life in Wayne Tower, either. Shouldering the bags, he headed up the stairs to the front entrance.

When Bruce exited the elevator into the private residence, Alfred Pennyworth got up from his desk to greet him. The desk was covered in papers. Though his official title was butler, Alfred did much more than that, overseeing the household, guiding Bruce's education, and handling communications from Wayne Industries with the skill and confidence of a former British Intelligence officer, which he was. And for the last seven years, since Thomas and Martha Wayne had been killed in a dark alley, he'd been the closest thing to a parent Bruce had known.

"Bruce!" he called to the teenager enthusiastically. "Welcome home! How was your spring semester?"

Shrugging, Bruce said, "Okay, I guess."

"Grades good?" Alfred asked, looking innocent.

"Think so," Bruce said, setting down his bags. "I didn't check."

Alfred smiled and held up a notebook computer. "I did. Straight A's. You made the Dean's List again."

"Yeah," Bruce mumbled, not seeming the least bit excited by this news. He always aced all his subjects with ease. Even if he didn't love boarding school, he enjoyed his classes and didn't mind working hard. In fact, he preferred burying himself in books and homework. It was easier to avoid socializing with his classmates that way. "Well, maybe I'll, um, put this stuff in my room. . . ." He started to pick up the bags he'd just set down.

"So," Alfred asked casually, "what are your plans for the summer?"

"Plans?" Bruce said, pushing a strand of dark hair off his forehead.

"Yes," Alfred said. "You're seventeen and you've got the summer free. What are you going to do? Travel? Join a sports team? Get a job? If you like, I'm sure I could arrange something at Wayne Industries."

Bruce looked out a window at the city below, uncomfortable with Alfred's questions. He wasn't sure *what* he wanted to do. Secretly, he craved action. Excitement. Even a little danger. But he wasn't about to admit that to Alfred or anyone else. One thing was certain, though: he didn't want to spend the summer working for his father's company. Or playing polo, or sailing, or any of the other things Gotham's young elites spent their time doing.

"I, uh, haven't really thought about it," he said. "But I will." He picked up the bags and headed down the hall to his room. "Definitely."

Chapter Two

A SECRET PROJECT

The next morning, Bruce woke up late. It felt good to sleep in. At boarding school, his days started early.

He looked around his room. Though Wayne Industries could easily afford to give him a big, fancy bedroom with all the luxurious touches a teenager could possibly want—giant TV, latest gaming console, even an indoor swimming pool with a slide and artificial waves—he'd chosen a small bedroom and kept everything simple. He liked to be able to find things quickly and easily, without searching through lots of drawers and closets.

Bruce pulled on workout clothes and took the elevator to Wayne Tower's well-equipped gym. His father had liked to keep in good physical shape. The room was filled with old-school dumbbells, punching bags, an ancient rowing machine, and even a heavy medicine ball. Only a few modern updates had been made since his death—an few elliptical machines and a treadmill. The gym smelled faintly of floor cleaner, metal polish, and sweat. Following a routine of his own design, Bruce made the rounds of all the weights and machines, lifting and pulling, working his muscles—not for bulk, but for lean strength and speed. As he did his sets of repetitions, he thought about Alfred's question. *What are your plans for the summer?* He figured he'd work out every day, but that wouldn't fill the whole summer.

"Good morning!" Alfred called, entering the gym. He, too, was dressed in workout clothes. "Thought you might like a session."

"Sure," Bruce agreed, setting down a barbell and heading toward a corner of the gym covered in mats.

"A session" meant practicing martial arts one on one. During his time in British Intelligence, Alfred had received extensive training in several fighting techniques, from karate to judo to tae kwon do. Over the years, he'd combined different skills into his own unique method of self-defense, and now he was passing it along to Bruce. Alfred liked to joke that he was teaching him "Brucejitsu." The term never failed to get a groan out of Bruce.

"Have you been keeping up your skills while you're at school?" Alfred asked as they squared off on the mats. "Found a practice partner?"

"Not really," Bruce admitted. "I'm pretty rusty. You're probably going to kick my butt."

"I'll do my best," Alfred replied with a sly smile. "Just remember, these skills are about inner strength and discipline, *not* kicking someone's butt, as you so eloquently put it."

But secretly, Bruce felt confident. Though he hadn't found anyone to spar with at school (or even *tried* to find anyone), he'd hit the gym pretty regularly and was getting stronger all the time. Besides, Alfred was in his forties. He'd better go easy on him. Bruce didn't want to accidentally hurt the old—

WHUMP! Bruce found himself lying on the mat, the wind knocked out of him.

"You're right," Alfred said, pulling him to his feet. "You *are* pretty rusty."

⚡

Later that day, feeling restless and at loose ends (and a little sore from the session), Bruce took an elevator all the way down to the basement of Wayne Tower. He switched on the lights and made his way past crates and boxes of papers and objects put into storage. In the far corner, behind an old furnace (long since made obsolete by a modern unit), was a plain door, barely visible in the shadows.

Bruce took out a key, unlocked the door, and opened it. Groping along the wall, he found the light switch and flipped it. Stone stairs led down to a cavernous space deep below the building. He turned and locked the door behind him. There was basically zero chance that anyone would follow him down here—but he liked to be sure.

Years earlier, Wayne Tower had been served by its own railway stop. The Wayne family had been able to ride their private train car right under the building, hop out, and climb the wide stairs into their home. The stop hadn't been used for decades, but Bruce had discovered it when he was thirteen, exploring every corner of Wayne Tower. There hadn't been much more down there than a set of rusty train tracks, a grand staircase, and four old-fashioned burned-out streetlights flanking the two sets of stairs, but he'd added work lights and made it his own space.

Without telling anyone.

To start, he had set up a small lab so he could run chemistry experiments without stinking up the building's living quarters. At first he'd pretty much randomly mixed chemicals to see what would happen. Nothing blew up. After reading about potentially deadly gases rising from ill-advised mixtures, Bruce had started carefully reproducing chemical experiments described in textbooks. Even as a hobbyist, Bruce had already become a relatively advanced chemist. He was even starting to successfully push the boundaries of what was in the books. Of course, his fortune and access to the equipment available at Wayne Industries gave him an advantage even as a hobbyist.

Eventually he had found that the experiments he enjoyed most were forensic—related to identifying substances found at crime scenes. He liked solving the mystery of what some gunk or goo really was. Though he didn't have access to crime scenes, now and then he'd scrape material off a bench or a sidewalk with a knife, seal it in a plastic bag from his pocket, and bring it back to his lab for analysis. Just for fun. (About nine times out of ten, the mysterious substance turned out to be chewing gum.)

But last summer, after he'd gotten his driver's license, he stored a different kind of project under the stairs of the old train stop. Maybe now he'd get back to it. Switching on his work lights, Bruce went straight to a long object and pulled off the dusty tarp he'd covered it with before heading to school in the fall. He smiled at what he saw.

A vintage sports car, the kind called a muscle car in the 1960s and '70s.

It wasn't in perfect shape. In fact, it looked pretty rough. But that was part of what Bruce liked about it. He saw its potential. He could make it his own.

Popping the hood, he got right to work, replacing parts, lubricating, tightening, adjusting—working with tools to turn the old car into something faster, sleeker, better. In his lab, he experimented with lubricants and fuels, seeing if he could improve them.

He couldn't explain it, even to himself, but for some reason Bruce felt an almost overwhelming need for speed. He didn't know where he wanted to go, but he knew he wanted to get there fast when the time came.

Maybe someday soon this car could take him there.

Chapter Three

EDWARD

At the orphanage, the boy in the choir who'd stared at Bruce Wayne was now attending high school. In seven years he'd grown, of course, but he was still scrawny, and still wore the same style of wire-rimmed aviator glasses he'd worn back then. He didn't sing in the choir anymore. The year his voice changed, he stopped singing. Music didn't really interest him anyway. Neither did school. He'd just finished another year at Gotham City

High School, and he'd advanced to the next grade—barely.

The boy's name was Edward Nashton. The only things that *did* interest him were puzzles. He always carried a book of crosswords or other puzzles, working on them with a stubby pencil whenever he got the chance. He'd even started trying to make his own puzzles, writing them down in cheap notebooks he hid under his narrow bed in the dorm.

He walked down the hallway of the orphanage to the main office. Younger kids ran by, chasing each other, thrilled to be free of school for the summer. A bigger guy, a year older than Edward, passed by, roughly bumping into his shoulder on purpose. "Watch where you're going, Ed-weird," he warned. His friends laughed. Ignoring them, Edward trudged down the hallway. He was used to the other orphans bullying him. He didn't care. He hated most of them anyway. Maybe all of them.

In the office, Edward signed out, letting the staff know he was leaving the building. As an older resident, he was free to leave as long as he said where he was going and went straight to a destination that had been approved. "This isn't a prison," the chief administrator always told them. "It's your home. And we're your family." Edward didn't believe a word of it. He had no family.

As he signed the sheet, a friendly woman named Bev behind the counter said, "Glad school's over for the summer, Edward?"

He looked up, not sure how to answer. You weren't supposed to say you hated school. But you were supposed to think summer was fun. "Maybe," he answered.

Bev smiled. "Where are you off to today? The park? The beach?"

To Edward, this seemed like an odd question. He had to write his destination on the sign-out sheet, so why was she asking him where he was going? All she had to do was look at the sheet. Was she trying to trick him? Catch him in a lie?

"I wrote it down," he said, pointing to the sheet. "Right here." He turned the sheet around so she could read it.

She peered down at the "Destination" column on the sign-out sheet. "'Job,'" she read. "Good for you, Edward! Where are you working?"

"All over," he said.

Bev looked confused. "You're working all over town? How many jobs do you have?"

Now it was Edward's turn to look confused. "I only have one job. Delivering food."

"Oh, I see," she said, nodding. "For whom?"

"People," he said. "Who want to eat some food."

Bev smiled. "I meant, which restaurant do you work for?"

"Fumento's," Edward answered. "Should I have written that on the sheet?"

"No, that's fine," she said, shaking her head. "I'm sure we have it on file."

"I've gotta go," he said, turning to leave. "I'll be late."

"Bye!" Bev called. "Be careful out there!"

He didn't answer. As he left, Edward looked at a framed picture on the wall. It showed Thomas Wayne with his wife and son standing in front of the orphanage choir on the day Wayne announced he was running for mayor. Edward glanced at this photo every time he came into the office. He saw himself in the choir, standing on the risers.

And he saw the famous son, Bruce Wayne. *He looked right at me that day,* Edward thought. *He smirked at me. Thought he was so much better than me.* He'd never met Bruce Wayne, but he saw his last name on the orphanage sign every day. Born so lucky—all that money. Probably didn't even appreciate being rich, since he'd been rich his whole life. Never knew anything different, like a fish not appreciating water. But if you didn't have it, you'd start to miss it in a hurry.

The other kids in the orphanage liked to joke about how rich Bruce was, describing how he'd used the rooms in the mansion when he'd lived there with his parents. "This was his closet," older residents would tell the youngest kids as they went into the biggest room in the house. In the dorms at night, they'd lie in their beds and say, "This whole room was just for his toys." Once they found an old suitcase in the basement. "Bruce's wallet," a kid joked.

"Bruce" became a code word for someone who was spoiled. If a distant relative sent some money to one of the orphans, everyone would say, "Man, you're such a Bruce."

Nobody sent money to Edward. He had to work hard for it, saving up for college tuition after he graduated from high school. He planned to study forensic accounting. When he read about it as a possible career, it sounded like solving puzzles. He figured the students wouldn't be like high school students. They'd leave him alone. But the classes were expensive. He'd have to deliver a lot of Italian food to pay for them.

Edward hurried to the garage, where he'd locked his bike to a rack. Someone had donated the used bike to the orphanage. It was old, and the gears slipped constantly. But it got him around town, even if the rack over the back tire rattled. He spun the numbers on the lock, pulled the chain through the spokes of the wheel, and wrapped it around the seat.

Then he climbed on and pedaled off to work, still thinking about that lucky rich kid, Bruce Wayne. *He's not spending all summer delivering food.* Just the thought of Bruce Wayne made him angry. He stood up on the pedals and pumped his legs as hard as he could until the chain slipped onto a smaller gear with a grinding sound. *Stupid piece of junk,* Edward thought.

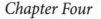

Chapter Four

THE BRUCE WAYNE

Lying on a mechanic's creeper under his muscle car, Bruce realized he needed a slightly bigger wrench. He reached into his tool belt, which he'd designed himself with loops and pockets so he didn't have to keep rolling out from under the car to search in his toolbox. He quickly found the right wrench by touch and tightened up a set of bolts.

He'd made several modifications to the car, all designed to increase its speed. A free-flow, large-diameter true dual exhaust system. A high-flow fuel pump. Large-diameter gas lines. The upgrades were all about getting more fuel and air into the engine while keeping the ratio right. He certainly didn't want to *blow* the engine. Just make it growl.

He rolled out from under the car, stood up, and wiped his greasy hands on a rag. Even though it was late at night, he decided to take his car out for its first test drive. He rolled it down off the rack, got in, and started the engine. It sounded good. Powerful but tuned—not out of control. Bruce slowly backed it out of his workspace, turned around, and drove away from the old train stop and onto the streets of Gotham City.

Though the car ran well, he kept thinking about more things he wanted to do to it: install performance cylinder heads and a supercharger. He could get the weight of the car down more, too, replacing the trunk and hood with carbon fiber versions. Maybe he'd try iridium spark plugs, though he wasn't convinced they'd increase the car's speed all that much. . . .

He zipped through the streets, accelerating through yellow lights and turning right if he hit a red light. He didn't really care where he went, though he tried to avoid traffic, sticking to streets with few cars and no stoplights. The car handled well, and there was no question about the power of its engine. Even when he pressed on the gas pedal lightly, the car leapt forward, going from a purr to a snarling growl that made him smile.

Bruce was heading toward the city limits, thinking maybe he'd drive out into the countryside, when he saw something in his rearview mirror.

Flashing red and blue lights.

Where had the cops come from? They must have hidden on a side road or in an alley, waiting for late-night joyriders breaking the speed limit. Bruce fit that description perfectly.

Letting out a frustrated sigh, Bruce slowed down, turned on his signal, and pulled over to the curb. The police car pulled up right behind him, its lights still flashing. As Bruce lowered his window, two police officers got out of the squad car and walked up. One of the cops looked at a street sign and said to his partner, "Hey, Mike. Is this still Eighth Avenue?"

"Far as I know, Sean," the other cop answered, playing along. "Why?"

"Oh, I don't know," Sean said. "The way this guy was driving, I thought maybe they'd changed it to the Indianapolis Motor Speedway."

Mike laughed.

"Sorry," Bruce mumbled. "Guess the car kind of got away from me."

"Got away from you?" Sean said. "Looks to me like you're still in it, with your foot on the gas. Your *heavy* foot on the gas."

Bruce silently handed his license, registration, and proof of insurance to the first officer, Mike. When the cop looked at the license, his eyes widened. "Bruce Wayne? *The* Bruce Wayne?"

"Bruce Wayne?" Sean said, raising his eyebrows. "Well, I'll tell you one thing—he can afford the ticket."

They both laughed. Bruce started to get annoyed. Why didn't they just give him a speeding ticket and get it over with?

Mike shook his head. "Busting rich kids isn't worth the paperwork. They just pay the tickets with their pocket change." He leaned down toward the driver's-side window. "Sit tight, Bruce. We'll be right back."

The two officers strolled back to their car and entered Bruce's license number into their computer. Then they returned to his car.

"You're clean," Mike said. "No record. So we're letting you off with a warning, okay?"

"Thank you," Bruce muttered. Inwardly, he chafed at what the officer had said. The cost of the ticket wouldn't mean anything to a Wayne . . . to him. No consequences. *But shouldn't there be consequences?* he asked himself.

"If you're gonna drive like that, you should be on a racetrack, not the streets of Gotham City," Mike continued, handing him back his license and papers.

"Slow down, kid," Sean said. "You're young. The world's your oyster. You got plenty of time. No need to be in such a hurry." Giving a small nod, Bruce rolled up the window. He wanted a lecture even less than he wanted a ticket. And he hated being called "kid."

As he slowly pulled away from the curb, Bruce shook his head, annoyed by the police officers' sarcasm. It continued to bother him that they hadn't given him a speeding ticket. He wasn't looking for special treatment just because he was rich. But couldn't they be doing better work than lurking on side streets, waiting to give speeding tickets to teenagers? Shouldn't they be out catching *real* criminals? The whole encounter rubbed Bruce the wrong way.

Something else one of the officers had said got him thinking, though. . . .

Racetrack.

Chapter Five

I KNOW YOU

The next day, Bruce drove out to a racetrack on the edge of the city. He was enjoying driving alone late at night, but he wanted to prove to himself that he'd put together a car that was fast enough to hold its own. He also wanted to test his driving skills, and he could only do that against other drivers. To know how you were progressing with your martial arts skills, you had to spar with a partner. To know how good your driving skills were, you had to race. That just made sense.

When he pulled into the parking lot, Bruce saw only a couple of other cars. It didn't seem like much was happening at the racetrack on a weekday afternoon. Things were quiet. Wandering around, he eventually found a door marked "Office." He opened it and went in.

Two guys looked up from their desks. "Can we help you?" one of them asked.

"Yeah," Bruce said. "I was wondering about your races."

"This time of year, they're just on the weekends," the second guy said. "The whole schedule's on the website." They turned back to their work.

"And, uh, how do you enter?" Bruce asked.

"You mean to drive?" the first guy asked, surprised.

"Yeah," Bruce said.

The second guy squinted at Bruce. "How old are you?"

He hesitated. He thought about lying, saying he was older than he was, but decided against it. He was pretty sure he'd have to show his driver's license at some point. "Seventeen," he said.

"Sorry, kid," the first guy said, shaking his head. "You gotta be at least eighteen to race here. State law. Why don't you just watch this year, and maybe give it a go next year? Tell you what, I think I've got some half-price admission coupons here somewhere." He started to rummage through the drawers of his desk.

The second guy was staring at Bruce. "Hey, I know who you are. I've seen your picture in the paper. You're that Bruce Wayne kid!"

When he heard the guy say his name—and "kid"—Bruce winced.

"Bruce Wayne!" the first guy said, looking up from a drawer. "I guess I can stop looking for those coupons. You don't need a coupon to buy a ticket to the races. You could just buy the whole track! Listen, if you do, I sure could use a raise."

The two guys chuckled. "Man," the first one said, "it's a good thing you're too young. I wouldn't want to be responsible for Bruce Wayne crashing on our racetrack. I'd never hear the end of it. Plus the city'd shut us down. Permanently."

"Oh, don't worry," the second guy told him. "His chauffeur does all the driving!" They both laughed.

Bruce felt heat rising in his face and neck. Certain he was turning bright red, flushed with anger and embarrassment, he turned and left without saying anything.

He let the door slam. Outside, he heard another burst of laughter, undoubtedly from another joke at his expense.

Back in his car, he was eager to drive away from the laughing men and their racetrack. Then, for just a second, he was tempted to find a way onto the track and take a few laps around the loop, showing them how fast he could go and how well he could handle the turns. They'd run out, flag him down, and tell him they'd been wrong—of course he could drive in their races. In fact, from what they'd just seen, they were pretty sure he could *win* their races!

But those thoughts flashed through his mind in an instant and were gone. He exited the parking lot, turning the opposite direction from the way he'd come. Since the racetrack was on the outskirts of Gotham City, in just a few minutes he was driving through the countryside, looking for empty, winding roads, roaring past farmland and patches of woods, alone with his thoughts.

The policemen the night before, the guys at the racetrack today—they'd all thought they knew exactly who Bruce Wayne was. Heir to a fortune. A billionaire. A spoiled rich kid who could have anything he wanted. Anything except his parents back.

He was sick and tired of people thinking they knew him when they didn't know him at all. Just because they recognized him and knew his name didn't mean they knew what he was thinking or feeling. They had no idea what he wanted. *He* wasn't even sure what he wanted.

The problem was being recognized. Bruce thought maybe he should do something about that. Find a way to disguise himself when he went out for one of his night drives.

Ahead of him, the country road straightened and flattened. He pressed harder on the pedal, and the car shot forward.

Chapter Six

DEX AND PAUL

The next night, when Bruce rolled his car out of the old train stop, he wore an army jacket, a black watch cap, and black work boots he'd found at a thrift shop, trying to make himself a little harder to recognize. It was impossible to keep track of every picture of him photographers had printed in newspapers and posted online, but he knew for sure that there weren't any pictures of him dressed like he was dressed tonight. For about two seconds, he'd considered a fake beard, but then laughed at the idea. Shades? Maybe on sunny days. But sunglasses wouldn't work for night driving. You needed your vision to be sharp if you were going to drive fast. And for now at least, he was doing all his driving at night, when Alfred was asleep.

He drove out onto the streets of the city. It was fun going fast in the countryside, but there were only two lanes. When Bruce encountered another car, he quickly passed it and drove on. The other driver usually slowed for him to pass. He wasn't interested in drivers that slowed down.

Cruising a four-lane avenue in the right lane, he saw a car ahead of him at a red stoplight. Bruce turned the wheel and slipped into the left lane, pulling up next to the car. It looked promising—an Italian sports car. Bruce gave his engine a little gas, revving the engine just a bit. Without turning his head, using his peripheral vision, he saw the other driver look over at him. He heard the Italian sports car's engine rev, louder than his.

Bruce smiled to himself.

With his hand on the knob of the gearshift (its shaft shortened so he could shift through the gears faster), Bruce watched the light for the cross street turn from green to yellow. The second the light in front of him changed from red to green, he peeled out, hitting the gas. So did the driver next to him.

They raced down the block, neck and neck, their engines roaring and whining as they shifted through the gears. At the next cross street, a stoplight was turning yellow. Bruce surged ahead, ripping through the intersection. The other driver thought better of this, hitting his brakes and stopping for the red light. As he sped down the street, Bruce saw the other car's headlights shrink into the distance. He grinned. That felt good— leaving 'em in the dust.

Keeping an eye out for police cars, Bruce wound around Gotham City, occasionally ending up at the front of a lane waiting for a stoplight to change. Sometimes the driver in the next lane would race. Mostly they wouldn't. Some even revved their engines, pointed forward like they wanted to race, but then slowly crept forward when the light turned green, laughing and shaking their heads, not wanting to risk getting a speeding ticket.

But after leaving one car at a light and zipping ahead, Bruce noticed something in his rearview mirror. A block or two back, a car was racing toward him, gaining fast. It wasn't a police car—there was no siren and no flashing lights. He couldn't identify the car's make or model, probably because it had been modified for speed. For one thing, the hood had been cut to make room for a shiny chrome supercharger.

Bruce kept pace, but the mystery car caught up with him. Instead of passing him, the driver matched his speed exactly, driving right alongside him. He glanced over to see who was driving.

He was surprised to see a girl about his age. She was pretty, with long brown hair. And she was smiling at him. She gestured for him to pull over. *Okay,* Bruce thought. *Why not?*

Bruce swung his car over to the curb and stopped. The girl parked in front of him, got out, and walked back to his car. He lowered the window.

"Hey," she said. "I like your car."

"Thanks."

"You do the custom work yourself?"

"Yeah," Bruce said. "Got a ways to go, though."

She smiled and shook her head. "It never ends. There's always another upgrade, another part. If you can afford it. Which I can't." She stuck out her hand. "I'm Dex. Technically, Dorothy Alexandra, but no one calls me that. Doesn't exactly scream out 'Gotham's fastest.'"

He shook her hand. She clearly expected him to tell her his name. He'd put on the jacket and the cap so no one would recognize him as an heir to billions, but he hadn't really thought about what he'd say if anyone asked his name. He quickly picked one, pretty much at random. "Paul," he said.

"Going to the race, Paul?"

Bruce looked puzzled. It was late. Were races still running at the speedway? "You mean at the track?"

She laughed. "No. Not the track." She gestured with an upturned palm toward the street. "Here. In Gotham. I thought you knew. The way you were driving, your car—I thought maybe you were headed to the race. Seems as though you like driving fast, from what I saw. And from what you've done to your car."

Now Bruce understood. She was talking about street racing. Tearing through the streets of Gotham City late at night, dodging the cops. Very illegal. He'd heard vague rumors about it. He knew he shouldn't have anything to do with that kind of activity. Alfred would kill him.

But Alfred didn't need to know. . . .

Chapter Seven

THRILLS

Bruce followed Dex to a part of the city he'd never been in before—mostly industrial, with no apartment buildings, restaurants, or shops. Some of the buildings looked abandoned. No one walked the sidewalks.

Dex drove fast, but Bruce kept up. He wondered if she was testing him. She'd warned him he probably wouldn't be able to race tonight. The other drivers would have to say it was okay first. Better to watch, see how it was done, and race next time, assuming they let him in.

In an empty lot, several cars were parked with their drivers standing around, talking and laughing. They looked like high school kids. Other cars were parked nearby with kids sitting on the hoods, ready to watch the fun. Dex pulled into the lot. Bruce parked next to her. They got out of their cars and walked toward the group of drivers.

"Hey, Dex," a guy called. "Ready to lose?"

She laughed. "To you? I don't think so." She gestured toward Bruce. "This is Paul. He's interested in our little extracurricular activity."

Another girl shook her head. "We're a full house already."

The guy next to her said, "If this gets too big, it'll be too easy for the cops to spot. They'll shut it down."

Dex shrugged. "He knows. I told him. Tonight, he'll watch. Maybe next time he'll race, if he gets here early or someone drops out."

"Does he talk?" the other girl asked. The drivers laughed.

Dex pretended to look puzzled. "I *think* so." She turned to Bruce. "Do you talk?"

"A little," Bruce said. "Sometimes."

The others smiled. "Good answer, Paul," a short guy with curly hair said, grinning. "We've already got plenty of big talkers. We don't really need another."

"Including you," another guy told the short guy. Everyone laughed, including him.

"Hey," the short guy said with an exaggerated shrug. "When you've got a lot of wisdom to impart, it would be selfish not to share it. Take transmissions, for example. Did you know that—"

Everyone groaned and rolled their eyes good-naturedly. Dex grabbed Bruce's arm and pulled him back toward their cars.

⚡

It had been a long shift for Edward, riding his creaky bicycle around the city delivering Italian food. As he pedaled through the dark streets, he'd notice the names on lit-up signs and turn them into puzzles in his head, thinking of rhymes and rearranging the letters to make different words. He'd do the same thing with the names of customers, coming up with anagrams—scrambled words and phrases using the same letters—on his way to their apartments and houses. Once he'd make the mistake of sharing one of his anagrams with a customer.

"Here's your lasagna, Mr. Alexander," he'd said. "By the way, did you know your last name is an anagram of 'Ax an elder?'"

Looking disturbed and slightly frightened, Mr. Alexander, a senior citizen, had taken his bag of food and shut the door without tipping Edward.

"Cheapskate," he'd muttered as he walked back to his bike.

Turning words and phrases into puzzles and riddles had become such a mental habit for Edward that he did it automatically. He couldn't deliver an order of rigatoni without thinking of a guy named Tony driving a rig. Every order of manicotti made him think of a man lying in a cot. Chicken alfredo always made him picture a guy afraid of a chicken, trembling with fear.

It was late, but he was finally riding back to the orphanage, done with work for the night. The tips had been pretty bad, but at least he had a few bucks in his pocket to bank for tuition. Even though his body was tired, his mind was still racing, thinking of rhymes and different meanings. As he cycled through the part of the city known as the Bowery, his brain churned out words. Bow like bow-wow. Bough like branch. Bow like take a bow. Bow like the front of a boat. Dowry. Flowery. Showery—

ERRRRRRT! A car, racing down the street, swerved to avoid Edward, its brakes squealing. Startled by the sound, Edward jerked his handlebars to the right and slammed into a parked car. *CRASH!* He fell off the bike, landing on the sidewalk. As he watched, blinking, more cars tore down the street. What was going on? Where were they all headed this late at night? And why didn't they watch where they were driving They could've killed him! They never stopped to make sure he was all right! It was like they hadn't even seen him. He felt invisible. He *always* felt invisible.

Edward stood up. He wasn't hurt badly—just a couple of scrapes. He picked up his bike and rolled it a foot or two. It seemed to be all right.

But he was furious, shaking with anger.

He'd seen the cars go to the end of the block and turn right, bunched close together, jockeying for position, trying to take the lead. He could still hear them after they turned the corner and drove out of sight, but their roar stopped soon after that. He figured they hadn't gone far. He got on his bike, wobbling a bit at first, and rode down the street in the direction they'd gone.

Edward found them just a few blocks away, parked in a lot. The drivers had climbed out of their cars and were congratulating a girl who seemed to have won the race, if that's what it was. They looked excited, laughing and talking loudly. Nearby, teenagers stood on their cars, applauding and cheering.

He recognized a few of the kids from Gotham City High School—rich kids whose parents could afford to buy them fast cars. Standing in the shadows a block away, watching, Edward grew even angrier. These kids had everything. Why would they risk their lives racing through the streets of the city at night? It was like they'd been handed everything he'd ever dreamed of having, and they'd just tossed it aside, moving on to the next shiny thing to smash and ruin.

They could race because they were born with money and the system on their side. If the cops arrested them, their parents would hire the city's best lawyers and get them out of it. Pay their fines. If they crashed their cars, their parents would buy them new ones. If they got hurt, the best doctors would fix them right up at the best hospitals.

The street race stood for everything Edward hated about the rich kids—their smug sense of superiority and entitlement. He'd like nothing more than to wipe those looks of self-satisfaction off their faces.

He turned away and pedaled toward the orphanage. But as he rode, he got an idea. What if he could somehow sabotage their race? Ruin it? Make them regret racing through the city at night, running a hardworking delivery guy off the road? They shouldn't be speeding anyway. That was breaking the law. It would serve them right to have their illegal race busted up. He could just call the cops, but that didn't seem satisfying somehow. They probably wouldn't listen to him, anyway. Maybe even make fun of him.

He'd thought lots of angry thoughts in his life, and he'd wished some terrible things on people who had teased him or pushed him around. Still, Edward had never actually done anything *really* bad. He'd barely broken any rules.

But now just the thought of doing something wrong—even something dangerously criminal—thrilled him.

Chapter Eight

YOU'RE IN

Bruce spent the next few days working on his car. He'd wake up early, hit the gym for an hour, and then head down to the old train stop, where he'd replace parts with upgrades until late at night. The next day, he'd get up and do it all again, occasionally taking the car out for quick test drives.

He had also observed the other race cars—their size, their weight, and any tell-tale signs the sounds gave him about their engines. He tried to get his car's weight down, taking out everything he didn't need and replacing panels with ones made from lighter material. Get more fuel into the engine. Get more air into the engine. Get the mix of fuel and air just right. Lubricate every part. Cut down the car's wind resistance as much as possible. All for speed. For now, he didn't really care what the car looked like.

Not everything went smoothly. Tools slipped off the heads of bolts. Parts didn't fit. More than once, Bruce spent hours installing a new part of the engine or the exhaust system only to decide it didn't really work— it didn't leave room for some other crucial piece. He'd have to take it out and start over with a different part, losing all those hours of work. It was a puzzle he was determined to solve.

Once or twice, he fantasized about walking into a car dealership and buying the fastest car they had. But that wouldn't be the same. Even though it was frustrating sometimes, working on the car and trying to get it just right, when he stopped at the end of the day and looked at what he'd done, he felt satisfied. Plunking down the money for a new car would never be as satisfying. And he had a feeling Dex would disapprove.

On the night of the next race, Bruce pulled on his black work boots, army jacket, and black cap. Then he rolled his car out of the train stop and drove to the starting point. He made sure he was there early so he'd have a better shot at being allowed to participate.

Dex was already there. When she saw him park and get out of his car, she walked over to him. "Paul! Good news! You're in!" She looked at the hood of his car and raised her eyebrows. "You added a supercharger since the last time we saw you."

Bruce nodded. For some reason, he had a little trouble thinking of things to say to Dex. He liked her. When he was by himself, he thought of what to talk about with her, but when he was with her, all those things flew out of his head.

Luckily, Dex had no trouble keeping the conversation going. "Well, let's see your handiwork. Pop the hood. We've got a little time before the race starts. Maybe I can fix whatever you messed up." She grinned.

Across the street, in a dark alley, Edward was watching the drivers, waiting for them to walk away from their souped-up cars so he could make his move—put his plan into action. He felt strangely calm and focused, like he was right where he ought to be, doing just what he ought to be doing. It made him feel powerful—he knew what was about to happen, and the rich kids had no idea.

"Sweet," Dex said, looking at the polished engine in Bruce's car. "Nice job. Can't wait to see this thing move."

"Thanks," Bruce said, proud of his work and happy to have Dex admire it.

"Drivers!" a girl named Hannah called from the other side of the parking lot. "Circle up!"

"That's us," Dex said. "Come on."

Bruce closed the hood and followed her over to the drivers gathering for last-minute instructions. There were about a dozen drivers, mostly local high school students.

As they walked toward each other, they joked and laughed, insulting each other's cars and bragging about their own. They acted as though they were just having fun, but every driver was dead set on winning the race.

"Okay," Hannah said when they'd all arrived. "First, ante up."

Dex had told Bruce about this part. It cost fifty bucks to drive in the race—cash. The winner got all the money. As they passed around a cloth bag with a drawstring, Bruce dropped in two twenties and a ten. He didn't want to seem like a guy who could easily put his hands on a fifty-dollar bill. He saw that Dex's fifty dollars included five singles.

Next, Hannah went over the rules. Basically, there weren't any. You got in your car, drove fast, cut other drivers off, followed the route (no shortcuts), and crossed the finish line. Whoever got there first won. You couldn't ram your car into other cars, but that was pretty much the only thing you weren't allowed to do. The drivers didn't think about the dangers. They were young. Invincible.

"Any questions?" Hannah asked. "New guy? Paul?"

Bruce shook his head. The short guy with the curly hair raised his hand and said, "I've got a question. When I win, what should I do with the money?"

The others laughed. A few made rude suggestions about what he should do with the money. Secretly, every driver there except for Bruce had thought about how they'd spend the cash when they won. Most of them planned to plow the money back into their cars, buying new parts. Like Dex had said, the upgrades never ended.

While the drivers were away from their cars getting Hannah's instructions, Edward slunk toward a black muscle car with a supercharger sticking out of the hood and crouched behind it. He reached in his pockets and pulled something out—something he'd specially prepared.

THE RACE

The drivers got in their cars and lined up along a straight black line someone had spray-painted across the parking lot. When they saw the drivers lining up, the kids watching honked their horns and cheered.

Bruce was thinking about the race route, driving parts of it in his mind. He'd gotten the route a few days before and practiced driving it a couple of times, noting its long, straight stretches, its short hops, and its tricky turns. It wound around the city, through the Bowery and the Financial District, past Arkham Asylum and the Iceberg Fish Co., and around Robinson Park. Some of it was familiar to Bruce, but some of it was new to him. The kids who'd laid out the route gave police stations a wide berth.

The drivers revved their engines, waiting for the signal to start.

Hannah walked the length of the starting line, lit up by the cars' headlights like a performer in a series of spotlights. She carried a checkered flag, which she was pointing at the ground. When she got past the last car, she turned and slowly raised the flag over her head, holding it high for all the drivers to see. It fluttered in the night breeze.

Then, with a quick slice through the air, she swept the flag down to her feet.

VROOOM! The drivers peeled out of the parking lot and into the street, burning rubber off their tires as they hit the gas. Hot clouds of exhaust shot out of their tailpipes. The spectators whooped and cheered.

Bruce was in the middle of the pack of cars. The street wasn't wide enough for them all to drive side by side, so they'd been forced into a line, with pairs and the occasional trio of cars next to each other. Whenever he got a chance, Bruce passed a car in front of him, trying to make his way to the front.

They roared through the city, passing empty lots and burned-out buildings, factories and landfills. The route stayed away from busy parts of the city, sticking to empty streets and boulevards whenever possible. Occasionally it cut through old parking lots with weeds growing from the cracked pavement, giving the drivers chances to pass each other.

Feeling the rush of racing through the city, Bruce went as fast as he could, slowing down only when necessary to navigate a turn. Other drivers tried to cut him off, weaving back and forth to stop him from passing them. But he soon got the knack of faking to one side and then swerving around to the other, passing car after car, one at a time.

About halfway through the course, Bruce was close to the lead. As far as he could tell, there was only one car in front of him.

Dex's car.

Every time he tried to get around her, she'd anticipate his move, matching his maneuvers, blocking him. And she was a bold driver, barely slowing down for turns, leaning into them and taking them as fast as she could.

But then, about three-fourths of the way through the route, Bruce saw a flash at the back of Dex's car. At first he thought maybe she'd installed a nitrous oxide tank and hit a button for an extra burst of speed. But then the flash turned into a flame, and the flame spread quickly. *BOOM!* Her engine blew, and her black muscle car careened off the street, hit a wall, and burst into flames.

BYE, PAUL

Bruce didn't hesitate. He pulled over next to Dex's burning car and jumped out. Inside, Dex was banging on the doors, trying to open them, but between the fire and the crash, they wouldn't open.

"Turn away from the window and cover your face!" Bruce shouted. Dex looked away. Her back to the window, she covered her face with her hands. Bruce raised his foot and smashed through the glass with his heavy black work boot. Working quickly, he kicked out as much of the glass as possible, reached through the window, and yanked Dex out. He carried her away from the car just as the fuel tank exploded. *BOOM!* The heat of it seared the back of his jacket and singed their hair.

Unaware of what was going on, the other drivers raced past Bruce's and Dex's cars, speeding for the finish line.

Dex coughed. "Are you okay?" Bruce asked.

"Yeah," Dex said, clearing her throat. "I'm okay. I wore my seatbelt like a good citizen should. Thank you for pulling me out."

"Sure," Bruce said. "No problem."

Dex smiled. "When I saw you were going to try to drive in those boots, I thought you were crazy, but now I'm glad. Just right for smashing windows." She looked at her burning car. "I wonder what happened. She was running so smooth. Did I blow the engine? Get the air-fuel ratio wrong?"

Shaking his head, Bruce said, "I don't think so. I saw a flash just before the fire started. It was toward the back of the car, not the engine. Almost like there was something in the tailpipe." He had a bad feeling—a tingling at the back of his neck.

"Flash?" Dex said. "That's weird." She looked at the burning remains of her black muscle car sadly. "Man. All the hours I spent on that car, up in flames. Literally."

"You'll get another," Bruce said.

"With what money?" Dex said. "I think I may be looking at the end of my brilliant racing career."

Bruce was looking at the car, too. The seats and the interior were still burning, but the flames at the back of the car had burned out. He got an idea.

"Do you mind if I get a quick sample from your tailpipe?" he asked Dex. "I'm just . . . curious."

"Sample?" she asked, puzzled. "Sure, knock yourself out. But be careful. Don't burn your hands. You should wear gloves."

"Good idea," he said. "Next time."

Bruce went to his car and got out the small emergency tool kit he kept in the back. Grabbing the longest wrench in the kit, he took off his black watch cap and stuck it on the wrench. Holding the wrench at arm's length to put as much distance as possible between him and the smoldering car, he stuck his knit cap in each of the twin exhaust pipes, quickly swabbing them. He carefully put the cap in his car, trying not to disturb whatever residue it had picked up from the tailpipes. He wished he had a plastic bag, but he'd taken everything unnecessary out of the car before heading to the race.

Dex stared at Bruce without his cap on. She furrowed her brow, thinking. "Hey, don't I know you?"

Bruce looked away, uncomfortable. "Of course you do. I'm Paul. You sure you're okay? Want me to take you to the emergency room?"

"No, I'm fine," she said. "Without your hat, you look familiar. Like I knew you before or something. Grade school, maybe?"

"Maybe," Bruce said. He saw other drivers heading toward them. They'd finished the race, noticed he and Dex were missing, and remembered the burning car they'd seen. Someone had called 911. Bruce heard a siren approaching. "I'm really glad you're okay, Dex," he said, getting back in his car. "I'll see you around."

"Wait!" Dex said.

But he was already driving off into the night. He didn't want to stay long enough for Dex to remember where she'd seen him before. And he definitely didn't want to risk getting his picture in the paper again, this time under a headline reading "Bruce Wayne Rescues

Girl from Burning Car in Illegal Street Race." If Alfred read that, he wouldn't let Bruce out of his sight for the rest of the summer. Probably make him take a super-boring job at Wayne Industries.

"Bye, Paul," Dex said with no one there to hear, watching his taillights fade in the distance. "Thanks for, you know, saving my life."

Back at the parking lot where the race started and ended, the crowd was breaking up. Word spread fast about what had happened to Dex's car, and they could hear the sirens coming. "So much for race night," one kid said sadly. Now that a car had caught on fire, the police would be on alert for any sign of street racing in Gotham. The drivers would have to lie low for a while—at least the rest of the summer. Or maybe forever.

Across the street, Edward watched the crowd scatter before the authorities arrived to investigate the accident. *Aww,* he thought. *Poor little rich kids! Did someone bust up your racing party? Too bad! I wonder who it could have been.*

He got on his rickety bike and rode all the way back to the orphanage, smiling.

Chapter Eleven

RUNNING

The next day, Bruce skipped his morning workout and went straight down to the old train stop. He took his black watch cap out of the plastic bag he'd stuck it in when he'd gotten home the night before. He set in on a light board and swung a magnifying work light over it. Then he examined the hat inch by inch, using tweezers to remove any foreign materials. He found a couple of wire fragments, which he examined under a microscope. Then he wiped the cap with white cotton pads. It yielded a powdery residue—possibly residue from the exhaust pipes.

After analyzing the residue and wires, Bruce was convinced that someone had stuck something in one of the tailpipes—something explosive. There might have even been some kind of timer wired to the explosive so it wouldn't go off right away. Or perhaps whoever had stuck the explosives in the pipe had used a slow-burning fuse to make sure Dex was driving her car when the explosion finally went off.

The more he thought about it, the angrier Bruce got. Someone had deliberately tried to blow up Dex's car with her in it! But who? One of the other drivers? Some kid who watched the races? The explosive device seemed too complicated to be just a prank.

Someone had meant to hurt Dex and make her crash into other drivers. Whoever did it could have been hoping for a massive pileup.

Bruce thought about reporting what he'd learned to the police. But there wasn't much to go on—most of the evidence had probably been burned. All he had was some residue and wire fragments. If he went to the cops, they'd ask what he'd been doing there, and the papers would be full of stories about Bruce Wayne driving in illegal street races.

Maybe he was wrong about someone targeting Dex specifically. Maybe someone just wanted to stop the races—someone mad at teenagers for roaring through the streets of the city at night, keeping them awake. But a bomb seemed like an absurdly extreme response. And he hadn't seen anyone there who didn't belong. Whoever did it had to be crazy.

Bruce's anger didn't go away. He wanted the person who'd stuck the explosive device in Dex's exhaust system to be punished. People like that shouldn't get away with their crimes.

For the millionth time, he thought about whoever had murdered his parents, still free, never caught, never punished.

He heard someone walking down the steps from the basement. He turned around and saw Alfred.

"Ah, so this is where you are," he said. "I missed you in the gym this morning."

"You know about this place?" Bruce asked, surprised.

Alfred smiled. "Bruce, it's my *job* to know what goes on in this household." He looked around the cavernous space, taking in the lights Bruce had set up, the worktables, the lab equipment, the microscope, the tools. "I like what you've done with the old train stop," he said, idly picking up a torque wrench. "Your very own man cave. Literally. Now, how was the race last night? Did you win?"

Bruce stared. "Race?"

"Yes," Alfred said. "You know, the illegal street race. The one you've been sneaking off to practice for. In this." He pulled the cover off Bruce's muscle car. Then he walked around the car, admiring Bruce's upgrades. "I had an old used car when I was your age. Tiny thing. Would've fit in the back seat of this car. Couldn't win a race with a tortoise. But I loved it."

"How did you know?" Bruce asked.

"I told you," Alfred said. "It's my job to know what goes on around here. Especially with you. Now, I need to know something else. Will you be doing more racing?"

Bruce shook his head. "No. I think the races are over."

"Good," Alfred said, peering at the supercharger emerging from the car's hood. "I don't much care for the idea of you getting arrested. The executives at Wayne Industries wouldn't be at all pleased. Not to mention the danger. If you got hurt—"

"I didn't," Bruce said. "No one did." He thought about Dex. That was close. But she was okay.

"Not yet," Alfred said. He looked Bruce in the eye. "Bruce, I'm not saying never take any risks, because that would be a waste of time. I know you will. I did, in my youth. In a way, life is about taking risks. But I hope you won't mind if I make just one observation."

"No, that's okay," Bruce said. "Go ahead. Observe." He'd actually expected Alfred to be angrier about the racing, so he was relieved when he seemed pretty chill about the whole thing.

Alfred tapped the muscle car. Bruce's work on the car had turned it into a thing of ferocious power and speed. He swallowed hard. Somehow the car was a brutal reminder of Thomas and Martha Wayne. "You can't get away from what happened to your parents. Neither of us can."

Bruce's eyes widened. Alfred rarely spoke of his parents' murder, knowing how painful the subject was for both of them. And the idea that Bruce's racing was somehow connected to that tragedy had never occurred to him.

"Instead of racing *away* from that terrible event," Alfred continued, "I think maybe it's time to start running *toward* something."

"Like what?" Bruce asked, confused.

Alfred shrugged and smiled stiffly. "I don't know. That's up to you—a mystery for you to solve." He pulled a key out of his pocket and held it up. "Don't worry— I'll lock the door behind me. Your man cave can remain our secret." He turned and headed back up the stairs, leaving Bruce alone.

For just a second, Bruce felt a little flash of anger. Maybe Alfred knew everything that was going on in Wayne Tower, but he didn't know everything going on inside Bruce's head. He wasn't running away from anything. He was just working on a car, speeding it up so he could drive fast. It didn't mean anything deep and dark and significant. Driving was just something to do during the summer. A way to kill time. In the fall, he'd go back to boarding school and forget all about his muscle car.

But Alfred had gotten him thinking about his parents again. About their killer still being out there somewhere, free, unpunished. He looked at the slides he'd examined under the microscope, evidence that someone had tampered with Dex's car and gotten away with it. It wasn't right.

Thinking of Dex, he remembered how he'd felt after pulling her out of the burning car. It was a good feeling.

Maybe even better than the feeling he got when he sped around another car. Yes, definitely better.

Ideas raced through Bruce's brain. Wanting to re-member them, he grabbed a blank notebook and a pen and sat down on the old stone steps of the train stop's staircase. He opened the notebook and wrote down the date. Then he wrote _Something To Run Toward_ and underlined it.

Part Two

Chapter Twelve

AN APPOINTMENT

The following year, after he graduated from boarding school at the top of his class, Bruce attended college. Actually, colleges. Thanks to Wayne Industries, paying for college was no problem, so he tried several, moving on to a different campus every time he grew bored with one. He kept changing his major—chemistry, physics, biology—and every time he picked a new field to explore, he found out where the best program was and switched to that university. Once or twice he even chose a school based on a single famous professor who taught there.

The colleges were located all over the world. Bruce liked traveling to new places and seeing new things, but he kept coming back to Gotham City. With all its problems, the gritty metropolis always tugged at him, pulling him home.

Building on the "Brucejitsu" Alfred had taught him, Bruce studied martial arts with masters in different countries, borrowing moves and tactics from each discipline, becoming a truly dangerous fighter. No matter where he was living, he always found a way to keep strengthening his body. Sometimes he worked out in sleek gyms with gleaming equipment. Sometimes he lifted milk jugs filled with sand.

Women liked him. He liked them, too, but he never stayed in one place long enough to form a lasting relationship. He wasn't sure he wanted one.

In the decade that passed, he thought about Dex every so often, but mostly he kept working toward his unknown goal.

⚡

Now in his late twenties, Bruce was back living in Wayne Tower. The building was still efficiently managed by Alfred. The butler persuaded Bruce to attend a few corporate meetings at Wayne Industries, but he found them incredibly dull. Business and making money didn't interest Bruce at all—maybe because he'd always had so much of it.

Still, Alfred kept trying. At lunch in the kitchen one day, he casually mentioned, "There's a board meeting this afternoon. I'm sure you'd be welcome."

"Can't make it, Alfred," Bruce said without looking up from an article in a forensics journal about gunshot residue.

"Oh?" Alfred said, mildly surprised. "An appointment of some sort?"

"Mm-hmm," Bruce said, absorbed in the article.

⚡

A new idea had formed in Bruce's mind. Somehow he could help bring justice to the streets of Gotham City. But he wasn't sure how though. Like Alfred had said, a mystery to solve. He just knew he wanted to do it in more direct way. He didn't just want to use Wayne wealth for charities and the like. The Wayne Foundation did plenty of that anyway.

As he walked through the bustling city streets, he felt energized by the idea. Just then someone called out for help—

Bruce saw that a mugger had snatched and elderly lady's purse. He was running straight toward Bruce. "My purse! Stop!" the woman cried. "Thief!"

Acting on instinct, Bruce stuck out his foot, tripping the mugger and sending him sprawling. The senior citizen's purse flew into the air as the mugger fell. Bruce caught it in one hand and politely returned it to the elderly woman. The mugger scrambled to his feet and ran off, cursing Bruce as he went.

"Thank you, young man," she said. Then she peered at his face. "Say, aren't you—"

Other people rushed up to help, all of them reacting in surprise as they recognized—

Bruce Wayne hurried away. It felt good to have helped a crime victim, but it was also hard to escape the cold, hard fact that he was Bruce Wayne. And it was difficult to disguise being a Wayne.

If he was going to bring the city's criminals to justice, he would have to work alone.

And then for some reason, he thought about the boots and jacket he had worn as Paul.

CHANGES

In the time since the summer of the street race, Edward Nashton had graduated from Gotham City High School somewhere near the bottom of his class. He didn't bother going to the graduation ceremony. No one was going to whoop when he walked across the stage.

In fact, he was pretty sure there'd be mocking chants of "ED-WEIRD!" He'd stayed at the orphanage that evening, writing more puzzles into his notebooks. By now, there was barely room for them all under his bed.

Eventually he saved enough from delivering Italian food to take the classes he needed to become a forensic accountant. Once he was certified, it took him a while to find a job. He didn't interview well. The whole process—earning the money, getting through the classes, passing the exams for certification, and landing a job—took years. But once Edward got an idea in his head, he stuck with it.

The work wasn't thrilling, but he was good at it, doggedly digging through numbers and accounts to find fraud. Living alone in a cheap apartment on the sketchy side of town, he drove a beat-up car to work. When the car was back in the shop for more repairs, he rode the bus, working puzzles in a book on his lap.

He had no friends at work.

Back at his apartment, he tried to escape from the loneliness of his life with more puzzles. Sometimes on weekends he'd go to garage sales and estate sales, collecting old greeting cards. He liked the ones with corny puns and riddles. But no matter how many puzzles he solved and created, he couldn't escape the feeling that life had pushed him aside, leaving him out, time and time again.

Edward wanted to change that.

One fall morning, Bruce and Alfred sat in the kitchen eating breakfast and reading the news on their laptops.

"Did you see they got Maroni?" Alfred asked.

"Yeah," Bruce said, nodding. "Finally."

Salvatore Maroni was the biggest criminal in Gotham City. For years everyone had known that he and his organization were behind most of the crime committed in the metropolis, but every time he'd been arrested, his lawyers had managed to get him off. As far as Bruce knew, he'd never been to prison.

"Think they'll make the charges stick this time?" Alfred said.

"You never know," Bruce admitted, "but it looks pretty good. The article says the cops seized 'mountains of hard evidence.' With what they've got, the district attorney thinks they'll be able to put Maroni away for life. That's good news for the city."

Alfred put down his cup of tea and sighed. "Yes, but Falcone's still out there."

"Falcone?" Bruce asked. The name sounded familiar.

"Carmine Falcone—the next kingpin," Alfred explained. "You knock one down and another pops up. Kind of like picking weeds out of a garden—if you don't dig up the roots, the weed will just grow back. In Gotham City, the roots of organized crime run very deep."

Finishing his cup of coffee, Bruce read the rest of the article about the Maroni arrest, thinking about what Alfred had said. He'd like to help dig up those deep roots.

As Bruce was closing his laptop, Alfred asked, "How did your appointment go the other day?"

"It was a bust," Bruce said, picking up the laptop.

"Ah," Alfred said sympathetically. "Sorry."

"That's okay. It was a long shot anyway. And that leaves me free to focus on another project." He stood up. "In fact, if you'll excuse me, I think I'll head down and get to work."

"Of course," Alfred said, hiding his surprise. "If there's anything I can do to help, please let me know."

"Thanks, Alfred."

Inside the elevator, Bruce rode down to the basement, and unlocked the door behind the old unused furnace.

Chapter Fourteen

A SUIT

The old train stop looked pretty similar to the way it had looked back when Bruce was in high school. He'd added a few computers and monitors to his workbenches, but the lighting was the same—dim and shadowy, the way Bruce liked it. His black muscle car was up on a metal platform. He tinkered with it sometimes, increasing its speed and power.

But now something else had grabbed his attention.

Bruce reached the bottom of the stone steps and walked over to an object about his size covered by a black cloth. He pulled off the cloth, careful not to snag the fabric on any rough edges.

It was a suit.

Not a business suit. Bruce had one of those that he wore when there was absolutely no getting out of a meeting at Wayne Industries. His navy-blue business suit was expensive, perfectly tailored, flattering, and comfortable. Bruce hated it.

This suit was more like a suit of armor. Its black material resembled metal plates that had been riveted together, like the hull of a ship. But it wasn't stiff like iron or steel. It was flexible, so that Bruce could still move in it, executing the martial arts moves he'd mastered over the years. The suit was made out of experimental, high-tech material unavailable to commercial manufacturers. Designed to fit Bruce's body perfectly, it hung on an old form once used by a professional tailor.

After stopping the mugger, Bruce had written his thoughts down in a notebook:

I'll take on the city's criminals alone so I won't put anyone else at risk. I'll need a disguise. I'll have to hide my face to keep people from recognizing me. A mask? And I'll need protection, like a bulletproof vest that covers my whole body. Made out of strong material—something highly durable. But it'll have to be flexible, so I can fight while I'm wearing it. Wayne Industries?

Though he had no interest in running Wayne Industries, he knew his father's company could give him access to the latest materials and technology. So he'd called the head of the appropriate department.

"Yes?" the department head had answered over the phone.

"Hi, this is Bruce Wayne."

"Haha. Hilarious."

"I'm not kidding. It's Bruce Wayne."

"Right," the skeptical employee said. "And I'm Albert Einstein."

Bruce thought of something. He tapped on the keyboard of his laptop. "I've just sent you a direct message through our secure system. You can use the information in the message, including my coded ID number, to confirm I'm who I say I am. Sorry, I should have thought of that before."

There was a pause while the department head checked his laptop. Bruce could hear him softly tapping the keys on the keyboard. Then he thought he heard a little gasp.

"Mr. Wayne, forgive me. My apologies."

"No," Bruce assured him. "I'm the one who should apologize."

"What can I do for you?"

"I'd like access to your department's research files. If you could just create a user account and send it to me through our secure channel, that'd be great. Once I have the account, I'll set up a new password myself."

"Of course," the employee said, sounding a little puzzled and alarmed. "Is there any particular area of our research you'd like to know more about?"

"No, I'm just taking a general interest," Bruce said. He didn't want to reveal his desire to learn about lightweight, flexible, bulletproof materials. That might lead to a lot of awkward questions.

Bruce's vague answer didn't reassure the head of the department one bit. "Mr. Wayne, is there anything wrong? Something you're concerned about?"

Bruce realized he'd scared him. The employee thought his department was being scrutinized by the owner of the company.

He'd have to be more careful in the future. He didn't

want to give anyone at Wayne Industries a heart attack.

"No," Bruce reassured him. "Nothing like that. This isn't an evaluation. This is just a . . . personal interest. Personal growth, you might say."

"Personal growth that requires access to all our research files?" the department head asked, still confused.

"Look, I didn't mean to worry you," Bruce said. "If you'd rather I didn't look at the files, I—"

"No, no, that's perfectly fine, Mr. Wayne," he said. "After all, in a very real sense, they're *your* files."

So Bruce had gotten the access he wanted. The confidential information in the company's databases was exactly what he needed to start building his suit. Unfortunately, word had spread that Bruce Wayne had expressed interest, for the first time anyone could remember, in the daily workings of Wayne Industries. When the corporate executives heard about his inquiry, they tried to pull Bruce in and get him more involved in running the company. But Bruce wasn't interested.

What interested him, at least for the moment, was building his suit. He grabbed a blowtorch, put on a welder's helmet, and went to work. He had ideas for several features that could give crooks nice little surprises.

In a way, working on the suit reminded him of working on his muscle car. Using the latest technology, he was trying to build up power while keeping the weight down.

Late that night, Bruce was still in the old train stop, scribbling a quick summary of his progress on the suit into a notebook. As he wrote, a bat fluttered past the light clipped to his worktable. He watched the little winged creature fly up to the ceiling of the cavernous stone space to join other bats, all hanging upside down.

Staring up at the bats, Bruce got an idea and started sketching a new design. It wasn't for now. But the thing taking shape on the paper got the wheels turning in his mind. . . .

Chapter Fifteen

THE POINT

Edward sat in the office break room eating his lunch. He brought the same lunch every day—sandwich, carrots, apple. There was only one problem with eating in the break room: other people. Mostly they left him alone to work on the crossword puzzle in the newspaper, quickly filling in the boxes with a pen.

But today a fellow accountant named Martin sat down across the table with his own lunch. He noticed

Edward with the newspaper and said, "Doing the crossword puzzle?"

Edward nodded without looking up.

"What's the point?" Martin asked.

Edward stared at him, frowning through his glasses. "What?"

"What's the point of it?" the accountant asked again. "The crossword puzzle. I just don't see the point of doing crossword puzzles. Somebody arranges a bunch of words in a box and makes up clues, and you guess what the words are."

"I don't guess," Edward corrected. "I know."

Martin smirked. "Okay, you *know*. The next day there's a new puzzle, so you solve that one. And the next day. And the next day. Spending all those hours getting the words right. I don't know—I guess words just don't interest me that much. I'm more of a numbers guy. Thought you would be, too. You know, being an accountant." He bit into his sandwich and chewed.

Edward looked him in the eye. "For a numbers guy, you sure use a lot of words."

Martin looked offended. "*Sorry*," he snapped, getting up from the table. "Just trying to be friendly. They

said you were weird. I guess they were right. No, wait—
I don't *guess*. I *know*."

He stomped out of the break room. Edward went
back to his crossword puzzle.

That night, alone in his apartment, Edward opened
a hardbound ledger and started writing down ideas for
puzzles. But then he stopped, remembering what the
jerk in the break room had asked. *What's the point?*

He looked at the shelves of his small apartment,
stuffed with his notebooks, ledgers, and boxes of old
greeting cards. What *was* the point?

Well, he thought, *what was the point of anything?*

Martin had called him weird. It was just like when
he was back in high school and the other students had
called him Ed-weird.

High school. His mind flashed on the summer when
he'd stuck the neat little explosive in the tailpipe of that
car, bringing the rich kids' street races to a fiery halt. He
smiled, remembering how good he'd felt that night, doing something wrong and getting away with it. Wiping
the smiles off the spoiled brats' faces.

Maybe he could get that feeling back again.

He opened a new ledger and started writing down
ideas. He'd show them the point—show *all* of them.

In a notebook labeled THE GOTHAM PROJECT, Bruce wrote: *Tonight, I'll start. I'm ready.*

He closed the notebook. He was dressed in an outfit similar to the one he'd worn back when he was racing his muscle car through the streets of the city—scuffed jacket, black knit watch cap, well-worn pants, and heavy black work boots. Anyone who saw him walking the streets would think he was a drifter, not the sole heir to the Wayne fortune.

Opening an old backpack he'd found in a thrift shop, he stuffed in his suit and gloves. He also wore a deep hood that enveloped his face in shadow. He also tossed in a tube of black camouflage makeup to smear around his eyes. He didn't know exactly how criminals would react to his costume, but the possibilities seemed good. If they were frightened, that was to his advantage. If they were confused, that was also to his advantage. And even if they were amused, they'd underestimate him—another advantage. He stuck his arms through the straps of the pack and pulled it snug against his back.

For the first time, he was going on a night patrol.

Putting on a helmet, Bruce climbed onto a black motorcycle from the 1960s and kick-started the engine. The bike was small, nimble, and surprisingly fast. It could take him anywhere he needed to go, small enough to slide through narrow alleys and passageways.

He rode out of the old train stop and into the autumn night under a full moon partly hidden by scudding clouds. He passed through a cemetery and onto a curving road that led into the center of the city. As he accelerated, he felt a strange mixture of nervous anticipation and calm satisfaction. It was good to finally begin the mission he'd spent so long thinking about and training for. He'd never been stronger, and he'd spent thousands of hours perfecting his skills as a fighter. It had been years since the last time Alfred had caught him off guard and slammed him to the mat.

In a dimly lit neighborhood on the edge of downtown, Bruce parked his motorcycle on the street and set out on foot. He figured walking was the best way to spot criminal activity.

In Gotham City, it didn't take long.

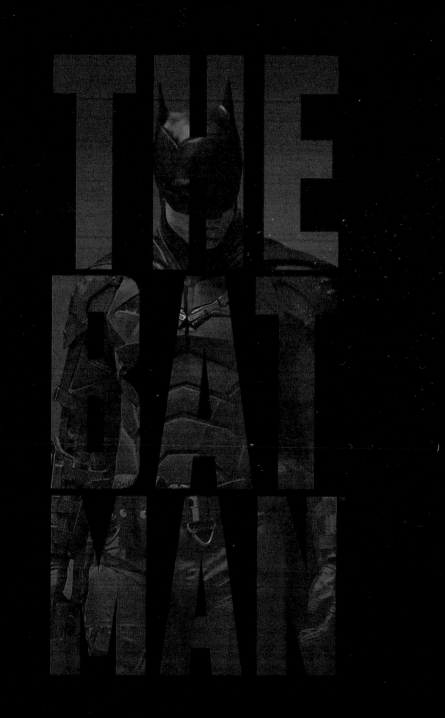

The Batman stalks the streets at night employing a lethal combination of mental mastery, physical strength, and expert technology on his journey to becoming Gotham City's symbol of hope.

Creating an intimidating silhouette amongst the city's shadows, the Batsuit is a protective armor that gives formidable tactical defense against criminals.

Selina Kyle is a mysterious figure who is quietly infiltrating Gotham City's criminal underbelly to further her own agenda.

But as Catwoman, Selina is also a
protective soul. She is more at home
with the city's strays than its citizens.

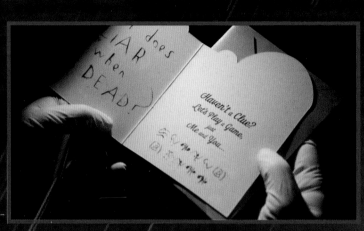

The Riddler is an enigmatic criminal who has devised a sinister series of puzzles and devices to entrap Gotham City's elite and publicly unmask the city's darkest truths.

The Batcave is situated deep beneath Wayne Tower. It's here that The Batman is able to stealthily hone his skills and develop genius new technologies in his mission to fight crime.

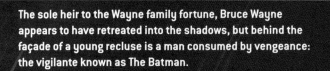

The sole heir to the Wayne family fortune, Bruce Wayne appears to have retreated into the shadows, but behind the façade of a young recluse is a man consumed by vengeance: the vigilante known as The Batman.

As Catwoman, Selina Kyle's fierce attitude and tenacious agility are the perfect tools to excel as a cat burglar.

Like The Batman, Catwoman isn't afraid to explore the darkest corners of Gotham City in the pursuit of justice.

The Batmobile is The Batman's awe-inspiring signature vehicle. Combining brute force with high-speed ferocity, this staggering feat of engineering provides him with the on-road muscle to chase down his fiercest foes.

Chapter Sixteen

ROBBERY

Light spilled out of a small jewelry store onto the sidewalk in front of the store. The sidewalk glittered from tiny flakes of mica, added when the concrete was poured decades ago. The store was closed, but the owners had left bright lights on, hoping to discourage thieves from breaking in.

Tonight, the owners' tactic wasn't working.

A figure dressed in black, his sweatshirt hood pulled up, skulked up to the jewelry store.

Looking around, he spotted no police.

Just a drifter down the block on the other side of the street.

As the thief turned his attention to the store's front door, Bruce ducked into an alley and peeled off his backpack. He quickly changed from his drifter disguise to his protective gear, smeared black camouflage make-up around his eyes, and pulled on his hood and gloves.

When he got close to the store, he expected to see the robber using some kind of tool to break in. Instead, the thief pulled out a small container, unscrewed the lid, and smeared something on the lock. Then he stepped back, aimed a remote control at the lock, and pressed a button. *FWWTT!*

With an acrid puff of smoke, the sticky explosive blew the lock off. The robber opened the door. *BRRRRINGGG!* An ear-piercing alarm blasted. Moving quickly, the thief smeared more explosive on the alarm and used his remote. *FWWTT!* Blown apart, the alarm went silent. The crook started scooping jewelry out of cases and into a bag.

Then a black-gloved hand gripped his arm.

The thief looked up and couldn't believe what he saw: a tall, imposing man dressed in a tight black suit of armor.

He wore long black gloves and heavy black boots. His face was covered by a mask connected to some kind of hood with sharp, pointed ears at the top. Only his mouth and chin were visible.

"Drop it," he said in a low voice, twisting the robber's arm.

Crying out in pain, the thief dropped the bag. Jewelry spilled out, scattering across the floor of the shop. "What are you?" he hissed. "Some kind of crazy security guard? Let go!"

The desperate criminal tried to twist loose, but Bruce held his arm tightly. Using his free hand, the robber pulled out his vial of explosive gel, smeared a glob of it on Bruce's glove, shoved the vial back in his pocket, and pulled out his remote.

Seeing that the criminal was about to ignite the explosive, Bruce released his grip and slid his hand out of his glove. *FWWTT!* With a puff of smoke, the gel reduced the heavy glove to shreds. Bruce had made the glove out of bulletproof material, so the substance, whatever it was, clearly could do some serious damage.

The second Bruce let go, the thief sprinted out of the store, leaving the jewelry behind. Bruce started to follow him but heard a police siren—the store's alarm had alerted the cops to a robbery in progress. He decided to disappear before the police arrived. Quickly gathering the remains of his glove, he dropped the fragments into a plastic evidence bag and vanished into the darkness just before the squad car arrived with its siren blaring.

After changing back into his drifter's disguise, Bruce rode his motorcycle to Wayne Tower to go over the night's events. *Not a bad start,* he thought as he wound through the cemetery.

He'd foiled the robbery, leaving all the jewelry in the store for the police to find. It wasn't a major crime—just a small-time hood hitting a low-rent jewelry store. But how had a minor criminal gotten his hands on such a high-tech explosive—compact, portable, adhesive, and easily ignited with a simple remote control? It had gotten him through the locked door, silenced the alarm, and covered his escape . . . but not before Bruce had slipped a tiny tracking chip into his loose jacket pocket during their brief struggle.

Chapter Seventeen

SMEAR IT ON, BLOW IT UP

Back in his workspace, Bruce carefully removed the fragments of his glove from the plastic evidence bag. Since he'd made the gloves himself out of experimental material, he knew their exact chemical composition. Any other chemicals he found probably came from the mysterious explosive.

His analysis did show chemicals not found in his gloves' material. When he searched databases of commercially available explosives containing those chemicals, he came up empty-handed. None of the explosives combined all the qualities of the thief's gel.

Staring at his monitor, Bruce considered his options. Since he'd planted the tracking device on the crook, he could follow its signal and bring him in. But before he did that, he wanted to know more about what he was dealing with.

He thought about calling an expert at Wayne Industries, but he didn't want to arouse more suspicions at the company. He'd already tried searching their research files but had failed to find a match for the explosive gel.

If small-time thieves were using a cutting-edge explosive in Gotham City, would the police already know about it?

He could use some help. And there was only one person he trusted completely.

↯

Alfred was in his study, going over household accounts. He looked up curiously when Bruce walked in.

"Alfred, do you have any contacts at the police department?" Bruce asked, coming right to the point.

"One or two," Alfred answered cautiously. "Are you in some kind of trouble?"

"No, nothing like that," Bruce assured him. "Just looking for answers to a couple of questions."

"Well, there's the commissioner, of course. Commissioner Savage."

Bruce shook his head. "Not that high up. I'm looking for someone smart, honest, ambitious—on the rise. Probably a detective."

Alfred raised his eyebrows slightly. "I'll make some inquiries."

Bruce turned to leave, but stopped and added, "Oh, and, um . . . leave my name out, please."

"Of course," Alfred promised, his brow furrowed. "*Discreet* inquiries."

Bruce smiled. "The best kind."

Later that day, Alfred passed a name along to Bruce: Lieutenant Janice Dure.

⚡

A sergeant dropped a large brown envelope on Dure's desk. "This came for you, Lieutenant."

Dure, a detective with black-rimmed glasses and short, practical hair, looked at the envelope. No stamps. No return address. "Who dropped it off?"

"A courier," the sergeant answered. "We scoped it—it's clean."

"Okay . . . ," Dure said, mildly intrigued. Maybe someone was sending anonymous tips on a case. The old joke around the station was that detectives were like waiters—they always wanted more tips.

She tore the envelope open and peered inside out of habit, checking for any white powder or another harmful substance. There were plenty of bad guys out there who would love to get even with her. All she saw were papers.

Dure pulled out the sheets and studied them. Someone had sent her chemical analyses of substances they claimed were part of a sophisticated explosive gel used at a crime scene in the city. The packet ended with a series of questions: *Is this explosive gel new? Have the Gotham City police found it at other crime sites? Where did it come from?*"

The sender promised to share any future information and gave instructions on where to drop off the answers to the questions.

Dure frowned, thinking. This "gel" didn't sound like any explosive she'd encountered before—on the streets or anywhere else. But she was no explosives expert. She decided to go see the bomb squad.

⚡

"Well, I'll tell you one thing," Officer Kim told Dure. "Whoever did this analysis knows what they're doing. It's impressive." She read through the pages carefully.

"What does it tell you?" Dure asked.

She sighed, thinking. "The specs match a gel I've heard of but have never actually seen. High-tech—light, portable, ignited electronically. Very advanced."

"Who makes it?"

"The military."

Dure raised her eyebrows.

"It's experimental," Kim continued. "Not available anywhere, as far as I know."

"Then where did the sender get the residue for this kind of analysis?"

Kim shrugged. "No idea. But if it came from a crime scene, that's really bad news. It means someone stole the formula from the military and started manufacturing it. It's basically a safecracker's dream—smear it on, blow it up. Quick and easy. Like locks don't exist anymore."

"And if someone's bringing it into Gotham?"

"They've gotta be stopped," Kim said firmly. "Or nobody's safe."

Chapter Eighteen

UNDER THE MASK

In the old train stop, Bruce read through the answers to his questions about the explosive gel. Lieutenant Dure had dropped them off where Bruce had specified and ended her note by writing, "If you find out anything more about this stuff, let me know. We'll handle it."

Bruce didn't mind sharing information, but he wasn't going to just stand by while the police handled everything. He wanted to find out who was bringing the gel into Gotham City and selling it to petty crooks.

It was time to go see the jewelry thief. On his laptop, he opened the application that showed the location of the tracking chip.

⚡

Wearing the same black hoodie, the thief walked down a dark block, heading toward another small jewelry store. Since it was the middle of the night, the commercial district was empty. But as the robber passed an alley, a voice said, *"Pssst."*

The crook turned and saw the same weirdly outfitted figure who'd ruined his last robbery attempt. *"You* again?" he gasped. "What do you want?"

"You," Bruce said, grabbing him with both gloved hands and yanking him into the alley. Spotting the thief reaching into the pocket of his hoodie, Bruce snatched the container of explosive gel out of his hands and held it up. "Where did you get this?"

"My grandma makes it," the thief sneered. "Old family recipe."

WHAM! Bruce slammed the criminal up against the brick wall of the alley.

"Okay, okay! Easy!" the crook pleaded. "I bought it."

"Who sold it to you?"

The thief shrugged. "We don't use names. Plus whoever it is wears a mask."

"What if I wanted to watch you buy some more gel?" Bruce asked. "Could you set that up?"

"No way," the criminal protested defiantly. Bruce lifted him up until his feet dangled off the ground and pressed him harder into the wall. "I mean," the thief gasped, "I guess I could."

⚡

Sometimes at night when he couldn't sleep, Edward drove around the city in his battered car, thinking about how he might get back that powerful feeling he'd enjoyed when he'd stuck the explosive in the muscle car's tailpipe. Often he followed the old routes he'd taken on his bicycle, delivering mediocre food for lousy tips.

One night, he drove down the familiar road that led back to the orphanage where he'd grown up. For years he'd avoided the old mansion, preferring not to think about his years there. But on this joyful night, he found himself parking out front, staring at the entrance, remembering.

He hated the place. He'd suffered there. Seeing the building again, he felt waves of loneliness and anger, a knot of pain growing in his stomach.

Then he got an idea. *What if it wasn't there anymore?*

⚡

Dressed in his black suit of armor, Bruce drove to the empty parking lot on the edge of downtown where the thief was supposed to meet the explosives supplier. He wanted to be ready for action. His car was ready, too—even faster and more powerful than when Bruce had raced it through the streets of Gotham City.

A block away from the parking lot, Bruce pulled over and switched off the engine. He spotted the thief, waiting nervously for the supplier.

A car pulled up, and the thief hurried to the driver's-side window. The robber handed over a wad of cash, and the driver passed a small canister to him through the window. Watching through binoculars, Bruce could see that the driver was wearing a mask. Then he saw the thief turn toward Bruce's car and jerk his head. He was ratting Bruce out to the supplier!

The supplier immediately took off, racing away from the parking lot, leaving the thief standing there. Bruce took off after the supplier's car, his tires screeching against the pavement. As he passed the thief, he reached through his window and snatched the canister of explosive gel out of his hands. "Hey!" the startled crook shouted.

Speeding through the streets of the city, Bruce got a faint tickle of memory. Something about the driver's style seemed familiar. Though the supplier's car was no match for Bruce's, it kept getting away, anticipating his moves, making sharp turns at the last second to escape being passed and blocked.

Finally, he saw his chance. On a wide, open stretch, he faked to the right. The supplier's car went right. Bruce floored it, zooming past the other car on the left, surging ahead, then cutting to the right, blocking the way. The other driver had to either crash into Bruce's car or stop.

ERRRRT! With its brakes squealing, the car skidded to a halt inches from Bruce's car. Bruce leapt out of his car, opened the other car's door, and pulled the driver out. He grabbed the driver's mask and pulled it off. Though it had been years since he'd last seen it, he recognized the face beneath the mask.

It was Dex.

Chapter Nineteen

A VISIT TO SMITTY

Dex had cut her brown hair shorter, but there was no mistaking her face. Bruce was so startled to see his fellow street racer again that he almost blurted out her name. He stopped himself from doing that, but he did loosen his grip on her arm.

Dex twisted free and jumped back into her car, which was still running. She backed up, spun around, and tore off into the night.

Bruce watched her go, still stunned. *Dex? Dex was bringing illegal explosives into the city and selling them to criminals?*

He couldn't believe it. Sure, the street racing she'd done in high school was illegal. But it was a long, dark road from joyriding at night to dealing in deadly explosives.

Had Dex taken that road?

↯

Back in his workspace, Bruce looked through his notebooks from the summer he'd met Dex. Most of his notes were about his car—parts replaced, lubricants tested, fuels tinkered with. But he'd also made a note of Dex's real name, Dorothy Alexandra. No last name.

Turning to his computer, Bruce quickly found digital versions of Gotham City High School's yearbooks and searched for "Dorothy Alexandra."

There it was: her senior picture. Her full name was Dorothy Alexandra "Dex" Starling. Next to her photo was her quote: *"Let's race!"*

Lieutenant Dure's phone rang. She answered, "Dure."

The voice on the other end of the line was rough, husky. "Lieutenant Dure. Thank you for the information about the explosive gel."

"You're welcome," Dure said. "I'd ask who you are, but I doubt you'd tell me."

"No," Bruce rasped. "But I do have a name for you."

Dure reached for a pad and pencil. "What is it?"

"Dorothy Alexandra Starling," Bruce said. "Goes by Dex."

"How is she connected to the explosive?"

Bruce ignored this question. "I wonder if you could run that name through the GCPD records for me."

"Look, I'm busy," Dure said gruffly. "I can't spend my time on errands for you. Especially since you won't even tell me your name."

"Just check one name," Bruce said. "That's all I'm asking. It could help stop this illegal explosives trade."

Sighing, Dure turned to her computer and typed in "Dorothy Alexandra Starling, aka Dex." A message popped onto the screen. "No results," she said. "She's not in the system."

Though he was disappointed to not get any information on Dex, Bruce was actually relieved her record was clean. Then he thought of something. "Try her as a relative."

Dure typed. This time, she got a result. "Her dad's in the system—locked up in a metropolitan correctional center. Bennett Starling. And she's in touch—never misses visitation hours."

"Thanks."

"Listen, you owe me," Dure said. But she realized the caller had hung up. "Big-time," she said to herself.

⚡

By the time Bruce reached the metropolitan correctional center in his drifter disguise, visiting hours were already underway. He thought about waiting to see if Dex would come out, but he was impatient to find out if she was already inside. If she wasn't, he was wasting valuable time he could be spending trying to track her down some other way. So he went inside.

The bored guard outside the visitors' room didn't look thrilled to see a scruffy guy in an old army jacket and a black watch cap approach him, but he was used to rough characters. "Yeah?" he grunted.

"Visitation?" Bruce said.

"Going on right now," the guard said. "You here to see someone?"

"Yeah."

"Okay, who?"

Bruce stared at the guard for a second. "Smith."

"Smith?" the guard asked. "Which one? We got a lot of Smiths."

"Goes by Smitty."

"We got a lot of those, too, buddy," the guard said. "You're gonna have to be more specific. Is that all you know? 'Smitty'?"

Bruce nodded. "Big guy." He was starting to think maybe coming inside to the visitors' room hadn't been such a great idea.

But to his surprise, the guard grinned. "Oh yeah, *that* Smitty." He picked up a phone and raised his chin toward the door into the room. "I'll buzz you in." *BZZZZRT.* The door unlocked. Bruce pulled it open and went through.

Several visitors were seated in front of thick glass

panels, using phones to talk to inmates on the other side of the glass. Toward the end of the row, Bruce spotted Dex, talking to an older inmate behind the glass. Luckily, the seat next to her was empty. Pulling his cap low, Bruce crossed the room and sat down, looking away so she wouldn't see his face. He thought the odds of her recognizing him as "Paul" after eleven years were slim, but he wanted to be careful anyway.

"Don't worry, Dad," Dex was saying. "I'm working on it. Just hang in there. It won't be too much longer."

Bruce couldn't hear what her father was saying on his end of the line, but he saw him smile at his daughter.

"I love you, too," she said. "Okay, I'll see you Friday."

As she got up to leave, a huge inmate was ushered into the room across the glass from Bruce. Looking puzzled, he plopped into a chair barely big enough to hold his massive girth, picked up the phone, and growled, "Who are you?"

"Sorry, Smitty," Bruce apologized. "Gotta go."

He got up and hurried after Dex as Smitty watched him leave, bewildered and a little disappointed.

Chapter Twenty

FOR MY LAWN MOWER

Outside the metropolitan correctional center, Dex briskly walked to her car and got in. Bruce hurried to his motorcycle, climbed on, and kick-started it. As Dex pulled out of the parking lot, he followed her, careful to leave some distance between them so she wouldn't spot him.

She drove out of the downtown area into a residential neighborhood where the suburban streets were lined with modest, one-story houses built decades before. In the middle of a block, Dex turned into an alley and parked in the third garage on the right, closing the door behind her.

From his motorcycle, Bruce noted the address.

⚡

That night, Dex left the house through the back door, carrying a small satchel. She locked the door, crossed the small backyard, and went into the garage. As she reached to press the button to open the garage door and turn on the light, a gloved hand gripped her right hand, stopping her. She gasped.

"Making another delivery?" a man said in a husky voice as he slipped the satchel off her left arm.

The overhead light stayed off, but the lights inside her car came on when she approached with the key fob in her pocket. By their dim light, she could make out a man in a black mask and some kind of armor. Looking around, she snatched the closest weapon at hand—a rake.

"Give me back that bag," Dex warned, lifting the rake.

"Or what?" Bruce asked, chuckling. "You'll rake me into a neat pile?"

Dex swung the rake at Bruce, aiming for his head, hoping to snag his mask and rip it off. Ducking, he grabbed the rake and yanked, pulling Dex closer. Keeping a careful hold on the satchel, he wrapped his powerful arms around her, trapping her. She struggled to break free.

"Listen," Bruce rasped. "I know you're running an illegal explosives operation."

"Running?" Dex said. "I'm not 'running' any operation. I'm just a delivery person."

Bruce turned her around so he could look her in the eye. "Why?" he asked. He still couldn't believe Dex was the kind of person who'd get involved in criminal activity. He'd only known her for a couple of nights when they were in high school, but she'd struck him as smart, direct, and honest.

"Why?" Dex repeated. "What do you mean, 'why'? Because crooks want the explosive, and they're willing to pay for it. Who are you, anyway? Another crook trying to muscle his way in?"

"I don't mean why is there an explosives trade," Bruce replied. "I mean why are *you* involved? Because of your father?"

Dex stared. "What do you know about my father?"

"I know he's in prison," Bruce said. "Is it his operation? Tell me the truth. Maybe I can help you, Dex."

Surprised the mysterious man knew her name, Dex tried to see his eyes in the dark shadow of his hood. Her instincts told her this guy wasn't a criminal. He didn't *sound* like a criminal. She took a deep breath and said, "The operation's being run by Reed 'Piggy' Porcello. He's all thug, and word on the streets is that he gets all his bad ideas from Oswald Cobblepot."

"Cobblepot?" Bruce asked. The name sounded familiar, but he couldn't place it.

"Yeah, Oswald Cobblepot," Dex said. "Some people call him the Penguin. These bad-guy types seem have a thing for nicknames. Penguin is one of Carmine Falcone's up-and-coming lieutenants. My guess is that he uses Porcello to make sure he doesn't get caught by his bosses sticking his hand too deep in the cookie jar. So Piggy framed my father and got him thrown in prison. If I help him move the gel into Gotham, he says he'll get my dad released. He only wants me because he knows I can drive. I race cars. My dad didn't do anything. He's never broken the law in his life."

Bruce decided to let go of Dex, trusting her not to take another swing at him. "Help me shut it down."

"Why should I do that?" she asked. "I don't even know you. Why should I trust a guy dressed up so I can't even see his face?"

Bruce took a step closer to her. "Because you don't want this experimental military explosive in the hands of criminals. You just want your father back. The police already know about the gel. They're moving in. Help me, and we'll get your dad out of prison. Refuse, and you'll both end up there."

Dex stood for a moment, thinking. She'd hated working for Porcello, but felt she had no choice because of her father. Now she tried listening to her instincts.

She nodded.

↯

On the opposite side of town from his apartment, Edward pulled into a gas station. He parked by the pump but went inside to pay. He wore a green jacket with the collar turned up, a floppy hat, sunglasses, and a white mask that covered his nose and mouth. Sliding a twenty-dollar bill toward the cashier, he said, "I'm going to fill my car at pump number two, but it'll probably only take a couple of gallons, so I'll come back for the change."

"What?" the cashier said, staring at his phone. "I can't understand you with that mask on."

"Sorry," Edward said, speaking louder. "I catch cold easily. Pump two."

The cashier nodded, still not looking up from his phone.

Edward went back outside, pumped a couple of gallons of gas into his tank, and returned to the cashier for his change. As the guy behind the counter silently pushed the change toward him, Edward cocked his head, pretending to remember something.

"Oh," he said a little too loudly. "Another thing. Do you have any of those plastic cans for storing gasoline? I need a new one. To store extra gas for my lawn mower."

Nodding again, the cashier pointed toward a shelf. Edward walked over and picked out a red container, then returned to the cashier. "I'm going to fill this," he explained. "For my lawn mower."

The cashier didn't say anything, still staring at his phone. Edward went back outside, filled the can with gasoline, and carefully set it in his trunk. Then he went back inside and paid.

And just like always, Edward had made exactly zero impression on the cashier.

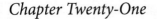

Chapter Twenty-One

NICE KICK

Late at night, Dex headed to the crumbling ruins of an abandoned factory on the edge of Gotham City. She drove around to the far side of the huge building and shut off her engine and lights.

Then she waited.

Before long, a truck arrived. It pulled up next to her. Dex grabbed a briefcase full of cash off her passenger seat, got out of the car, and walked around to the driver's-side window. The tinted window lowered, revealing a tall, thickly muscled man behind the wheel.

"You're late," she told him.

The driver ignored this. "Got the money?"

Dex patted the briefcase. "Right here." She handed it to him through the window. "I'll pop the trunk. You can load the stuff there."

The man opened the case. "First I count."

"You don't trust Porcello?"

"I don't trust nobody." He started counting the cash.

Dex took a step back. From a nearby door in the old factory, a figure in black armor slipped out of the shadows. Crouching low, he darted over to the back of the truck. Then he made his way to the driver's-side door, keeping close to the ground.

The driver was absorbed in counting the bundles of cash. Suddenly, his door flew open. Two gloved hands reached in, grabbed the driver, and yanked him out of the truck, throwing him to the pavement. Bruce leapt into the truck and started to drive off. Dex was supposed to jump in her car and drive away, too.

But as Bruce looked in his side mirror to make sure Dex got away, he saw the driver on the ground reach into his pocket, pull something out, and aim it at the truck.

A remote control.

In the dorm rooms at the orphanage, everyone was asleep.

BRRRRINNNG! BRRRRINNNG! BRRRRINNNG!

As the fire alarm went off, sleepy orphans climbed out of their beds. The youngest ones jumped up, ready to run out of the old mansion. The older ones took their time. "Relax," they told the younger residents. "It's just another false alarm. Some jerk pulled the alarm again. There's no fire."

They were right. There was no fire. Yet.

The night caregivers hustled the children out of the building and onto the lawn. In just a few minutes, the building was empty.

Except for the person who'd pulled the alarm.

From his years of living there, Edward knew exactly where the adults would guide the kids out of the building. Kids had pulled the alarm hundreds of times, and the response to the fire alarm had remained exactly the same. And since he knew the escape path they'd follow, he knew where to hide to avoid them as they filed out.

The difference this time was that the orphans

wouldn't come back in. They'd never have to live in the old Wayne mansion again. *No one would.*

Carrying his red plastic gas can, he quickly made his way to the front office. The old photo still hung on the wall in the same spot. *They'd never dare take down this picture,* he thought. *It's got the great Thomas Wayne in it, their benefactor, their saint. And his beloved son, Bruce.* He reached up, lifted the framed photo off its nail, and carefully put it in his backpack between sheets of bubble wrap.

Then he unscrewed the cap on his can of gasoline, put in the nozzle, and got to work.

⚡

Just as the driver was about to press the button on the remote control, igniting the explosives in the back of the truck Bruce was driving . . . *WHACK!* Dex kicked the remote control out of his hand. It flew in the air, landed on the concrete, and smashed into pieces.

The explosives didn't ignite.

Furious, the big driver got to his feet and lunged at Dex, probably thinking if he took her hostage, he could get back his truck with its load of cargo and briefcase of cash. He didn't know who the guy in the black suit was, but he figured he must be working with the woman.

Dex dodged the guy and ran. *VROOOM!* Bruce roared up in the truck, putting it between the driver and Dex. The driver reached toward the truck's door, hoping to get at the masked man in the driver's seat, but Bruce swung the door open, slamming it into him and knocking him out cold.

Bruce jumped out and quickly secured the thug's hands behind his back with zip ties. He called to Dex, "You okay?"

"Yeah," she said. "I'm okay. Thanks."

"Good," he said, hoisting the guy over his shoulder and carrying him toward the back of the truck. "Nice kick."

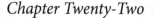

Chapter Twenty-Two

BUSTED

Bruce slammed the back door of the truck closed and locked it. He turned and saw Dex standing with her arms folded. "Thanks," he told her. "I'm driving this to the police."

"What about my dad?" Dex asked. "When Porcello finds out about this, he's going to be furious. He'll never get my father released from prison."

"If you're right about Porcello running this operation without Falcone's knowledge, he's going to be in big trouble with his boss. He'll have to shut the whole thing down. That includes framing your dad and keeping him in prison."

"You'd better be right," Dex said.

Bruce took a step closer to her. "Don't worry. You did the right thing. We'll get your dad out of prison."

"Who's 'we'?" Dex asked. "Do you work for the cops?"

"I work for Gotham City," Bruce said, climbing into the truck.

Lieutenant Dure was working late again. Her phone rang. "Dure."

"Got a delivery for you," the voice on the other end said. "Out front." The call ended.

Dure got up from her chair, walked down the hallway, and stepped outside. A truck was in a no-parking zone in front of Gotham City Police Headquarters. She approached the truck cautiously. No one was in it.

But someone had scratched something into the driver's-side door. She leaned over, peering at the scratch marks. She made out the words *"Look in back."*

The keys were in the door. Dure took them out, walked around to the back of the truck, and opened it. She saw a large, unconscious man with his hands zip-tied behind his back. Behind him were sealed boxes. The detective opened one. It was filled with metal canisters and remote controls. Explosives.

After Dure had gotten officers to start processing the suspect and the evidence, she returned to her office. A sergeant knocked on the door and stuck his head in. "Lieutenant? This came for you by courier." He held up an envelope.

Inside, Dure found papers describing the illegal explosives operation, including Porcello's involvement and information about a man named Bennett Starling, apparently framed by the thug. With this information, the evidence in the truck, and the testimony of the zip-tied suspect (who would probably give up plenty of information to save his own skin), Dure felt confident she could trace the explosives back to whoever was making them and shut down the whole thing. She smiled, satisfied. This was big.

But then, at the bottom of the last page, Lieutenant Dure spotted something puzzling . . . a small, simple drawing of a bat.

In a dark room at the Shoreline Lofts, a man stood by a pool table, idly rolling a cue ball down to the far end of the table. It bounced off the cushion and rolled straight back to his hand every time. He caught the ball and rolled it again.

There was a soft knock at the door. Oswald Cobblepot, wearing an expensive pinstriped suit, opened it.

The man who entered looked tough and confident, but there was small sheen of perspiration on his forehead. He eyed the man in the striped suit and nodded.

"Hey, Oswald," he said quietly. And then in a louder voice, he spoke to the man at the pool table. "You wanted to see me, boss?"

"Yeah, Piggy," Cobblepot said. "Come on in. The boss will be with you in a second."

"The club's doing good tonight," Porcello told the man, who was Carmine Falcone. Piggy grinned nervously. He didn't like the silence. "Of course, it does good every night."

"Right," Falcone said warmly as though accepting a compliment. "Now, I got a question for you."

"Shoot," Porcello said, approaching on the pool table.

Taking a cue from a rack on the wall, Falcone said, "Why shouldn't I take this cue stick and play a dozen games of Nine Ball on your thick head?"

Porcello turned pale. "What? Wh-wh-why would you do that?"

"Your little side project," Falcone said. "That fancy explosive."

For just a second, Porcello considered denying his involvement. But the look on his boss's face told him this wouldn't work. "It—it was just a trial operation," he stammered. "T-t-to see how it'd go. Once it was really up and running, I was going to tell you all about it, I swear."

Porcello looked over at Cobblepot, hoping for some backup, but the Penguin looked anywhere in the room but at him. Porcello continued, "S-s-say the word and I'll shut the whole thing down. Tonight."

"Too late," Falcone snapped, running his finger along the cue's smooth, polished wood. "The cops already shut it down. Word is they're gonna spring that old man you framed, too. A real mess."

"Look, boss," Porcello pleaded. "I made a mistake."

"A *big* mistake."

"A *big* mistake," Cobblepot agreed. Falcone shot him a look, and the Penguin knew better than to speak again.

Porcello stammered, "It—it—it won't happen again."

"It better not," Falcone warned, his jaw clenched as he wrung the cue menacingly. After a moment, he set the cue down on the table. "I'll make sure the cops don't get you for this one. Pull some strings. Next time, I don't know. Now get out."

"Thank you, sir." Porcello turned and left, scowling at Cobblepot as he passed.

"Some guys . . . right, boss?" Cobblepot said, chuckling to lighten the mood now that Piggy was gone.

But Falcone didn't smile back. He stared right into Cobblepot's eyes with a terrible, unknowable blackness. It made Cobblepot swallow hard. He wished he were anywhere but that room.

"Some guys, indeed . . . *Penguin*," Falcone replied as his smile returned. He picked up the cue ball and resumed rolling it across the pool table.

Chapter Twenty-Three

RESOLUTIONS

The firemen put out the last smoldering embers at the orphanage. Since the alarm had gone off, they'd gotten there in time to stop the fire before it burned the mansion to the ground. But the building was a total loss. No orphan would ever live there again.

Edward let a few days go by before he drove to the burned relic late one night. As he looked at the charred remains, he felt vaguely unsatisfied. He'd enjoyed setting the fire, but no one knew he was the one who'd done it. Of course, it was good to get away with the crime—to avoid being arrested and thrown in prison. But no one had learned anything. No one had gotten his *point*. Nothing important had really *changed* in this lousy, corrupt city.

And he hadn't gotten any credit. He was still invisible, a nobody.

Then something interesting occurred to Edward. *What if I sent riddles with my crimes?*

↯

At breakfast, Bruce and Alfred ate in silence, reading the Gotham City newspaper on their laptops.

Then Alfred broke the silence. "Interesting story here."

Bruce thought he knew the one Alfred meant. He'd just read it himself. But he picked a different story at random. "The one about repairing potholes downtown?"

"No," Alfred said, smiling. "The one about the police breaking up a trade in illegal explosives. Seems most of the credit goes to a Lieutenant Dure."

"Good for her," Bruce said, staring at his laptop.

"Say, wasn't that the detective whose name I gave you recently?"

Bruce nodded slowly. "Sounds familiar. Yes, I think so."

"How did that work out?"

Bruce looked up from his laptop. "How did what work out?"

"Whatever you needed Dure's name for?"

"Oh, that," Bruce said, reaching for his coffee mug. "Dead end."

Sighing, Alfred set down his cup of tea. "Bruce, I know."

Bruce frowned. "Know what?"

"Your . . . project," Alfred said. "What you're doing at night. And, for what it's worth, I . . . I do not approve, but I understand. Gotham City has been in such a decline since your parents died—especially your father. He loved this city. And I guess you do, too. Maybe it needs something—or someone—to shake things up. But what you are doing is so dangerous. For you. For your family's legacy."

The two men stared at each other.

"I don't suppose I can talk you out of this . . . course of action?" Alfred asked.

Bruce shook his head imperceptibly.

Alfred sighed.

Bruce said firmly, "Remind me to change the locks on the basement door."

"Certainly, sir," Alfred said, and straightened himself. "I will take care of it."

Bruce nodded as Alfred turned and left. Now that the secret had been shared, it was somehow more real. This thing . . . this project . . . this course of action, as Alfred had put it. It was what he was going to do.

It was what he was going to become.

⚡

A few nights later, on an empty stretch of road, the masked figure waited, leaning against his motorcycle in the shadows. In the distance, a pair of headlights cut the darkness as a car approached. The car pulled up and stopped smoothly. Dex got out and walked over to him.

"So you're as good as your word," Dex said without preamble. "Given the new evidence, the police reopened my father's case. Some hotshot lawyer from Wayne Industries is doing pro-bono work on the case and is making sure everything happens super-quick.

She's even going to make sure nothing goes on my record. And we got a big fat check from some sort of Wayne charity to help us make a fresh start. So it seems I have an angel looking after me now."

"Sometimes things work out," her black-clad cohort agreed. The words hung in the air, and then he awkwardly added, "And it's good that we made a difference. We make a good team."

Dex thought it over, giving the starless Gotham sky her attention for a moment.

"My dad and I need to get away. Maybe Metropolis. I hear LexCorp Race Team is taking on new mechanics. Or maybe I should just go back to school. Either way, maybe that fancy Wayne lawyer could put in a good word for me."

The man nodded. "Take care of yourself."

Dex understood that whatever this had been was over now. She got back in her car and pull out onto the road.

She looked in the rearview mirror, but the man was already gone. . . .

Epilogue

A couple of years later, on a rainy Halloween night, Bruce prowled the streets of Gotham City dressed in his army jacket and knit cap, carrying his backpack. Though he looked aimless, his wandering was part of a carefully planned routine.

As he later wrote in a journal:

Notes & Observations (Gotham Project)
Year Two
A second year of nights has turned me into a nocturnal animal. My senses are heightened now. I can almost smell them.

"Them" meant criminals. Gotham City was full of them. "But they don't know where I am," Bruce would write.

In a dim alley, Bruce opened his backpack and pulled out a tube of black camouflage paint. He quickly smeared the paint around his eyes, then reached into the pack for a black hood with long, pointed ears.

On the roof of an abandoned, half-built skyscraper downtown, a rusted searchlight shot its beam into the rainy night sky. Attached to the center of its lens was a dark shape: a metal bat with its wings outstretched.

As Bruce would write later that night, "A signal now, for when I'm needed. But when the light hits the sky, it's not just a call. It's a *warning*. To *them*."

A masked figure dressed in black stepped into the dim light of Gotham City.

"I *am* the shadows. I am vengeance. I am . . ."

The Batman.